Confessi

Leïla Sebbar

Confessions
of a Madman

A Novel
Translated by Rachel Crovello

 DALKEY ARCHIVE PRESS

Despite its mission to support French literature in translation, and in particular to to support the cause and well-being of translators, CNL (Centre national du livre) would not provide support for the translator of this book, and this at a time when there has been a substantial decrease in the number of books being translated into English. Dalkey Archive urges CNL to return to its mission of aiding translators.

Originally published as *La Confession d'un fou* by Bleu autour in 2011.

©2011 by Leïla Sebbar.
Translation copyright ©2016 by Rachel Crovello
First edition, 2016

Library of Congress Cataloging-in-Publication Data

Names: Sebbar, Leïla, author. | Crovello, Rachel, translator.
Title: *Confessions of a madman* / by Leïla Sebbar ; translated by Rachel Crovello.
Other titles: *Confession d'un fou*. English
Description: First edition. | Victoria, TX : Dalkey Archive Press, 2016.
Identifiers: LCCN 2015044154 | ISBN 9781564787606 (pbk. : acid-free paper)
Classification: LCC PQ2679.E244 C6613 2016 | DDC 843/.914--dc23
LC record available at http://lccn.loc.gov/2015044154

Partially funded by the Illinois Arts Council, a state agency

www.dalkeyarchive.com
Victoria, TX / McLean, IL / London / Dublin

Dalkey Archive Press publications are, in part, made possible through the support of the University of Houston-Victoria and its programs in creative writing, publishing, and translation.

Cover: Art by Eric Longfellow

Printed on permanent / durable acid-free paper

We don't know where the man disappeared to.

The room is like a cell. The red carnations at the edge of the window have not yet wilted, the dirt is still damp.

A woman is sleeping on the bed.

In an ancient trunk made of cedar wood, there is a kind of journal written by the man. It's of no use to the police because it is undated.

The following is legible on the notebook cover, outlined in India ink: "Confidential."

1

My father never held me in his arms.

2

They killed my father.

His body was thrown under the tree in the middle of the square, his hands tied behind his back. He was barefoot. His beautiful riding boots—my father went everywhere by horse—did they take his shoes before shooting him? An armed soldier stood guard.

Behind the small wall of dry rocks, I watched. I didn't move, I didn't eat, and I didn't drink the whole time the body of my father was left under the tree. The soldiers took shifts to prevent us from approaching.

My mother was still young and beautiful; I didn't recognize her. Her hair in a mess, her cheeks scratched, no belt to tie her dress; her servants weaved sophisticated belts just for her.

The servants—I heard them from behind the threads of the weaving loom—they said that the master, who had barely jumped off his horse after returning from the steppe— what was he doing all those days he disappeared? Pursuing falconry, at war, fighting with guerrillas?—they said that he visited his wife, knelt down to greet her, swiftly untied her most beautiful belt, threw it across the room as if it were a long silk ribbon, and carried his beloved in his arms to the large leather bed, an inheritance from the Ottoman Empire.

My mother left the house at night, she watched with me, but the nights were very black. She didn't see anything. I described to her in a low voice: the brown stain around his head, the bare feet, the hands tied behind his back, the stiff fingers. She cried softly.

The body of my father was not given to my mother. The swollen and stinking body. The soldiers hunted the scavengers. The flies flew in a swarm, green and thick; the soldiers could do nothing against the flies. Before the dawn of the fifth day, while her servants were sleeping, my mother left the house for the village square. The surveillance was discreet, but she was watched; she was never left alone, as the master's aristocratic line would not allow it. After jumping over the heavy door, my mother ran toward the slain body, the vigorous and courageous man, the magnificent husband. The body of my father had disappeared. She began to scream, and despite the soldiers' threats she continued for a long time, they tried to drag her toward the post, she struggled, they gave up, they let her scream, crouched against the wall. I was so weak that I couldn't manage to bring her back to the house, and I fell asleep to her cries.

3

My mother always spoke of the body of my father without a grave.

She used to tell me, "If you find out anything, whatever you do, don't forget it, tell me, I must know, even a little finger, a hand, if the body stepped on a mine, who knows what happened, tell me, I promise you I won't cry, I won't cry."

My mother did not cry again. But during the following years she believed that I would one day reveal the secret of the body that disappeared. My mother never gave up. The eternal loved one was not dead. She sent her servants everywhere they might hear the murmured words that would speak the truth. Into the livestock markets, dressed as citizens. Into the hammams where women chat indiscriminately. Into the cabarets and the cafés where women don't go, where they disguised themselves as boys. Upon their return, my mother, waiting impatiently since morning, listened to their reports. The first few days, they found nothing, and my mother protested, swore to God that he was alive, that they had a sacred mission toward the masters that had fed them from the cradle, without whom they would be dead or beggars or worse . . . The following days, the servants fought with each other to be able to speak, they said more and more, they made things up, my mother believed them, she believed the most extravagant rumors circulated by one and then the other, she believed everything. Until one day she said, "Silence! I don't want to hear you anymore . . . I forbid you from leaving. You'll stay in the house. I'll go alone, everywhere, without rest, and I will know."

Until her death, the servants gathered in the vagabond's house, and my mother became known as "the madwoman of the Plateaus."

I did not look for the body of my father.

4

I was forewarned that it would be difficult.

I don't believe it.

5

I was told to change my hiding place every day. I'm not hunted, I'm the one who hunts.

I have a room, which belonged to my father, in the red-light district. Everyone knows, I am known, I know everyone. I say "Hello, how are you?" and I am greeted simply. I speak to no one, I have but one friend, my company is not sought out, I'm not talkative; who loves silence? Men who do not talk are feared, they're taken for crazy people.

I am not crazy, I do not speak, I am not feared.

6

My mother, what did she know of my father?

A distant cousin, his horseback riding exploits were praised, he loved horses; he ruined his own father. When his father died, he began working for an uncle who was a butcher. He was good at chopping up meat, he worked well, the uncle thought about leaving his butcher shop to him, the business was good, he had no children, he was proud of his nephew's dexterity in handling the knife, he gave him a beautiful dagger inherited from his grandfather.

But one day the nephew recognized a horse carcass slung over the shoulder of the assistant who delivered the meat, he began acting crazy, he threw himself at the young employee, he threatened to kill him. The young man fled, leaving the piece of meat on the sidewalk, and the nephew, my father—he had not yet met my mother—he insulted his stunned uncle, knocked over tables, threw the decorated hooks across the store and into the street, he thrust all around him with the giant knife as if it were a sword, the uncle called for help, he was brought under control, he disappeared.

He disappeared until the day he married his second cousin, she was young, very young, he loved her eyes—black like the savage lights of the high plateaus before the storm. With the dowry, he bought horses that he trained. He ruined my mother. He was a great horseman. My mother loved him.

7

My father rode my mother like the most beautiful of his mares, the white one, and I was born.

8

I knew that I would succeed, I succeeded, it was perfect. I was congratulated, I don't like being congratulated.

9

Sometimes I visit a woman, I've been going to the same one for a long time; she's young, a little fearful, her skin is very white and smooth, she has clear, sad eyes. I don't want to know why she's here. She doesn't speak, and it's good.

I chose her among the women in this district, women of cabarets and closed clandestine houses—the pleasure houses are reserved for the dignitaries—people smoke hashish and the musicians know how to dance.

I sit in a chair next to the bed, she is standing near the mirrored armoire, I speak a little, nothing important, she looks at me. I stand, I caress her cheeks, her round shoulders, then I'm off.

10

My father didn't raise me, he raised and trained horses, he didn't teach me anything. He went far away, I begged to accompany him, he always refused, he said, "Later, later . . . you're too young." I grew up. He still said "You're too young."

I'm afraid of horses.

11

I was chosen because I kill with a blade.

12

The room of the woman I have been visiting almost daily for the past three months smells of citron and musk. I asked her to stop perfuming herself with musk, because the scent nauseates me. I almost vomited one evening when I smashed an oily, fragile bottle of it on the Persian rug that a lover gave her before leaving the country, he was chased out, I know it, he terrorized girls, pathetic bastard.

I prefer the citron.

I sniff her pale thigh, that acidic scent from the inside, clear like water from a fountain, she laughs, I lick her, a happy laugh.

I stop by unannounced. If she doesn't open the door because a man is there, she knows I won't come back.

13

The razor has a horn handle. I stole it from my father, before his death.

14

When the soldiers threw the body onto the hard-packed dirt at the foot of the tree, the only tree in the square, the most beautiful tree, the largest in the village, I ran with the other boys until we reached the gunmen who stopped us at a good distance. The boys stopped shouting, frozen in a line behind the soldiers, and they looked at me. I thought they were mocking me. I turned my head toward the arrangement under the tree, and I saw my father. He wasn't wearing his riding boots. I didn't smell my father's scent, the thick tan leather worn by the sweat and the races on the high plateaus, his childhood region, the land of his lovers.

At nightfall a few days later, when I woke up and my mother was no longer screaming, she brought me to the cemetery, to the family resting place.

I'm not afraid of cemeteries. I often accompanied my grandmother and her sisters. They said to my second cousins that followed them, "You, you stay in the house. You can come when you're older."

"And him, why does he go with you?"

"He's a boy, it's different."

"He's a child, like us."

"Yes. But he's a boy."

The cousins repeated, "That's unfair."

And the old ladies repeated, "That's the way it is."

I went with them, the cemetery wasn't far, the pathway from the house to the tomb is simple, no barriers—the walls were erected later; it reeked of geranium. They chatted joyously, the day at the cemetery was neither a day of sadness nor a day of silence.

Near a tomb at the foot of a centenary cedar or yew tree, I don't remember which, a tomb worn with lime, my mother ordered me to dig. She had brought a small pickaxe. At first I refused. To dig for an absent death . . . I resisted, she hit me. The pickaxe was small, the ground was dry and hard, my mother helped me with a stick and then with her hands, we dug for three days, at dusk, at the hour when people are eating at home.

The grave remains empty. It will be for my mother. Not for me, I won't die in that wretched village that I abandoned forever; when I left, my mother knew that I would not return.

My mother went crazy, I learned this from the peddlers that wandered aimlessly while I went on my way. I remember one day I walked a long time; when my feet collided with the familiar doorstep I understood that I had arrived at my mother's house. I didn't think, I looked at the beautiful door, the copper door knocker, and I left the village. In the cafés at the edge of the paths, I heard about "the madwoman of the Plateaus." I didn't realize at first that the domino players were talking about my mother. When they talked in all the cafés about the house left to the servants, the disappearance of the heir, the dishonorable punishment, the leader of the revolt deprived of a grave, and the desperate spouse wandering immodestly along the Plateaus, I recognized my mother.

I thought that she wouldn't reach the town.

15

The woman that smells like citron is surprised at how much time I spend standing at my window. I don't hide behind the wooden venetian blinds or the folds of a curtain to observe; my window has no curtain. I don't try to surprise anyone, I observe while standing; if it rains I close the window, if not I leave it open. I can spend several hours like this at the window. Often I don't look at anything, I think or I don't think, I stand there, that's all.

On the edge of the windowsill, red, fine carnations with curly petals grow, they're called Sweet Williams, they were there when I moved into this room.

16

When I use my knife or my razor, the razor is sometimes more efficient, I cut a red carnation and put it in my buttonhole.

17

The trough was close to the house, at the other end of the yard. The courtyard fountain was too delicate for a man, my mother said, "It's a woman's fountain, very precious." My father's black stallion, which my father always forbade me from approaching and touching despite my pleading, went by itself up to the trough, where my father joined it with his shaving items. Early in the mornings he shaved there. He sat down on a rock, filled a basin with clear water, and shaved while singing. He used the razor with the horn handle, he sharpened it well, I watched his precise movements, hard and fast. At the end of the song the horse put his muzzle on my father's shoulder and my father looked in the mirror while laughing. He stood up and said, "The horse, he loves me."

I said, "My mother too, and me too." He didn't listen, he just jumped onto the stallion, which he rode bareback, and left at a gallop, as if he were going very far, into the deserts.

At the house my mother prepared coffee in the courtyard, near the women's fountain. I didn't cry, but my mother told me, "I know, he's leaving, perhaps he won't return, he's a brute . . . Don't cry."

"I'm not crying. My father doesn't love us."

My mother persisted, for her own sake. "He loves us . . . like a brute."

18

When I arrived I smelled the musk.

When the woman approached me, I insulted her, if she had spoken I would have hit her, she said nothing and I left.

19

In town I walk like an animal, missing neither the tiniest pebble nor the thinnest scrubby tuft of flower. I'm like an animal that knows without error the vegetation and the invisible unevenness of the ground that evades the eye of the hunter. I walk, familiar, happy. I wasn't born in this village and yet it's my village, my land; it hasn't been a stranger, it has loved me since the first step, it was timid. So was I.

I wander the village with the same brutal fervor as when, as a child, I would walk for hours in the Plateaus, alone, never getting lost. My mother waited for me like she waited for my father, patiently. She loved us, she never gave up. She knew that men and their sons stray from the woman's home. When I returned after running away, far away to the fragrant rocks, they smelled like rockrose and absinthe, I sat down on a small wooden bench against the wall, in the shade of the pomegranate tree, and I closed my eyes until hearing the noise of my mother filling a basin with hot water.

The light brass of the bowl bangs against the red brass of the basin, I open my eyes. My mother splashes my feet with hot water, too hot. I protest. She says, "You're crazy . . . Why make yourself bleed?"

"I didn't feel anything."

My mother looks at me. "You too are a brute." The towel is soft. The blood makes uneven stains. My mother says, "You won't move for three days. I'll watch over you . . ." She laughs, "You, who can watch over you?"

My mother prohibits the servants from carrying out these actions; she alone, wife and mother, can wash the feet of her master and of her son, "the light of her eye." She says while laughing at the servants, "You'll never know how beautiful my husband's feet are!"

20

I discovered caves, my lairs, I haven't told anyone about them. The town also offered me its caves against the storms. The storms are ferocious in certain seasons, the caves protected me each time. They were fresh bedrooms for an afternoon nap.

Many times, from the mound where I was crouching to rub my feet, I thought I saw my father galloping in the distance. Looking down at the ground, I told myself, "I'm going to raise my head and I won't believe it, but it will be my father. Standing on the stirrups, he'll raise the old saber inherited from an ancestor higher than the palomino's head, he'll shout my name, I'll think, "I'm mistaken, this horseman is not my father." And my father dismounts his horse, he looks at me, my feet are bleeding, he leans toward me, "It's nothing. I have also run on these rocks and my feet have bled. It's nothing, my young one." He touches my hair, I don't get up, I'm in pain. My father jumps onto his horse, he turns his back on the village. I follow him for a long time with my eyes."

I went almost every day to the place where I thought I saw my father, where he was supposed to face me, I would have run to him, he would have taken me in his arms.

My father never held me in his arms.

21

As if I were the only one to accomplish these feats with the knife or with the razor, they speak to me.

I think I'm going to leave town.

22

I didn't leave town.

23

I took the woman who smells like citron—the musk disappeared from her room—to a secret cave in the town.

She is docile. She is beautiful.

She says that she loves me, it's all that she says. She speaks little, as I prefer. She says that she loves me, but I don't believe her. She likes to say those words, to say them, simply, to repeat them to a man who doesn't mistreat her like the men do with the prostitutes that are too young and are waiting for love.

24

For the first time I thought I was going to miss my chance.

25

I didn't stay long in the cave with the woman. She is young, she is beautiful, infatuated maybe, tender and skilled, her skin is warm, under her hair that covers her she is petite, her hair curls down to her waist. She has learned to act this way, as a fine, stupid girl.

26

I didn't see the woman at her place again. I no longer want to play with her hair.

I won't see her again.

27

I was told, "He is a high dignitary. If you fail him, he will kill you." I'm not a contract killer. I'm not a terrorist.

From now on I want to act alone.

28

My mother tells me an old story. She says that it's a very old story about the beginning of the world, nobody knows the exact date, not even the scholars. Slowly she repeats, "Abraham took the knife to cut his son's throat."

I'm forced to take a siesta, I don't sleep, I become bored, sometimes I scream as if I were having a nightmare, my mother hears me, she arrives immediately. I make something up: "I was on the black palomino, it was galloping, I yelled into its ear, it threw me off and flattened my throat with its hoof." As if I had spoken the truth, I cried. My mother takes me in her arms. "My partridge, my falcon, I know that you prefer 'falcon' . . . Don't cry, I'm here."

She sits at the foot of the bed at twilight and speaks in a low voice, I hear her, "Abraham took the knife to cut his son's throat." I say nothing, I listen to the story of Abraham and his son Ishmael.

29

I ordered the woman to leave the district, I don't want to see her anymore, not in the street, nor at my window, nor at the coffee shop. The madam protested, she didn't want to lose her most beautiful girl. I didn't have to threaten her, she obeyed, I accompanied the woman to a taxi with her two suitcases.

I don't know where she took refuge. I simply

recommended a house outside of the town; there's no short-
age of beautiful dwellings, the madam is rich. She prefers the
old town district, she'll die in her house of birth surrounded
by her girls, those who are not pretty enough for the secret
towns where the dignitaries and the grateful Authorities,
spoiled by her, amuse themselves, invisible, sequestered in
the pleasure houses.

I know the blue house. I know that everything is possible
until you get killed. So it is said, and I believe it.

30

The servants used to chat behind the blossoming pomegranate trees. They talk about the master of the blue house, they
call him Sardanapale.

31

I went into a library in town. Sometimes I spend the siesta
hours there in a dilapidated room that smells of oak, a familiar odor. The tree in the square, it was an oak tree. It smells
like dust and mold, the books had gotten wet when the cellar
flooded, there was nobody to take care of them. It smells like
decomposing paper, it smells like silence.

I looked in a dictionary of great men or famous men, I
don't remember which. I found Sardanapale and, illustrated,
The death of Sardanapale. The room is poorly lit, colors are
distinguishable, but not precise shapes, I'll return with an
electric lamp.

At home, I don't have any books out in plain sight.

32

The best slingshots are made from the wood of the pomegranate tree.

33

As soon as my father returned from hunting, my mother panicked at the sight of the kitchen tiles covered with fur and feather game, still warm, sometimes still alive. I rushed to the shouts of the women gathered at the door who assisted in showing off the fabulous hunt. Each man that entered threw his loot on the pile that reached up to the height of a seven-year-old child.

My mother distributed the already butchered beasts to the women, overwhelmed and nauseated by the odor of wild game blood. It was necessary to work quickly. The women feathered the edible birds without talons on the spot, the more experienced women butchered and dressed the game at the back of the yard, the place was always the same, the pile of animal skins.

I chose the animals that were still breathing. I hid them in my shoulder bag and I ran alone, far from the women and the dogs, until I reached an isolated shed. I locked myself in and slit the throat of the red and white partridges, the wild pigeons, the pheasants, sometimes a hare or a bustard. The men kept the wild boars for themselves.

There were no gazelles where my father hunted. We lived too far away from the sands. I've never gone to the desert. I like the town. It gives refuge to the crazy people, the desert isolates them. It is said that the desert is beautiful. I don't like the desert.

My father and the other hunters threw the game onto the green tiles and disappeared. I never knew where they went.

34

The madam's messenger told me that the woman locked up in the blue villa is sick, very sick, and that she wants to see me.

35

At the library I saw the cruel and refined prince stretched out on a giant bed wearing traditional clothing. Is he going to die? I've seen naked women stabbed by men. I've seen a large black man in a turban fighting with a thoroughbred. Will he slit the horse's throat on the tyrant's bed?

I passed the white light of the electric lamp over each detail: the jewelry, the white arms, the helmets, the drapery. The debauched despot's face looked melancholic to me.

36

I thought the body under the oak tree in the middle of the square belonged to a hunter killed by a gunshot during the course of the chase. The soldiers had thrown him here in the village so that the families could come identify one of their own.

My father, alive, I almost never saw. Never three days in a row.

It was hot during the day and at night. They left the body of my father to slowly rot for five days. His horse wasn't with him. Had they killed it and thrown it into a ravine? Had they shot my father on horseback, or had he been on foot? My mother knew nothing. The other men had disappeared or had been killed and abandoned in the ravines of the Plateaus.

Why did the body of my father, and only his, lie at the foot of the oak tree, to be discovered? Was he a leader and I didn't know about it? My father didn't speak to me. When I saw my father, I asked him questions, but he didn't respond, or he said, "You'll understand later."

It's too late. The green flies around his face and the wound, the green flies on the stains of black blood, dung flies. My father didn't speak to me.

They prevented my mother from covering the body with the shroud that she held between her breasts like a precious possession. My mother folded the shroud at the foot of her bed, sure that one day the men of the family would rediscover the body of the beloved cavalryman. My mother didn't know that my father, the best hunter this side of the desert, the head of the revolt, was deadly with a knife. He hunted with guns, not knives. But everyone also says that he was more skilled than a butcher at slaughtering the ceremonial sheep. When he was still a child, his father allowed him to slaughter for certain families because he didn't ask for money. His mother didn't know about it, and they say she wouldn't have allowed him to work as a butcher.

What I know of my father, I learned through rumors. He became a person of legend. People told of his exploits with the knife, his bravery, his dexterity, how he scared people. He's dead . . . Perhaps it's better this way. What would he have done in a time of peace? I repeatedly heard, "If it hadn't involved traitors and enemies of the people, he would have been a monster . . . But he was a hero."

I didn't know that my father was a hero. He was already dead, his body long devoured by vultures and hyenas. And my mother kept the shroud clean, ironed, folded, at the foot of her ottoman bed, beside the copper bars. She hadn't yet abandoned the grand house to wander along the Plateaus, from village to village, sleeping in caves and cemeteries, eating bread and dates on the doorsteps of marabouts. Has she tasted the honey that the pious women leave there on their march to the Saint's tomb? My mother loved the honey from her gardens. My father had hired an old beekeeper who taught her to collect honey, both gold and red. I prefer acacia honey.

37

I don't know if I'll go to the blue house.

38

I don't fear death.

39

I know a garden at the edge of the town, behind the hills of the upper town, far from the area where I live. I go there on foot, I like to walk, I don't go by taxi, bus, or car, even when I leave town for the Plateaus. The beekeeper is like a friend. We barely speak. He lets me accompany him to his beehives. I watch him work, but he makes me wear a suit, gloves, and the mask that protects the head and neck.

I've also raised bees, they gave the best honey. My mother had fashioned me a jute canvas frock cut from large grain sacks from the cellar where she stored supplies. As for the mask, I fashioned one with pieces of metallic mosquito net. My mother knitted the gloves.

Often I return home with a pot of acacia honey. I nourish myself with honey, bread, and coffee. My mother always told my father that he drank too much coffee, that coffee would make him die before his time. Did the soldiers offer one last cup of coffee to my father before killing him? Maybe a last cigarette? My father didn't smoke, I don't smoke.

Thanks to the Sweet Williams, bees stop by my window. I don't shoo them away.

40

I went to the blue house.

The garden smells like cypress and mimosa. In the third courtyard there is a fountain with statues—mermaids, tritons, dolphins; this excess of carved, tormented rock prevents me from seeing and hearing the water.

It's a rich house, not very beautiful. I was led to the sick woman's bedroom. A servant brought coffee and left us alone. She's not very sick, she exaggerates a natural melancholy.

She asked me to take her away. I told her that it's impossible because a woman is always taken away on a galloping horse, preferably a black one, and I'm afraid of horses. She vowed she would kill herself; her poison, she said, doesn't leave her. I offered her my razor with the horn handle, and she withdrew, terrified. She must have thought . . .

She looked at me, disoriented, and I headed toward the bedroom door. She said, "Take me away." I left. I will no longer return.

41

Why does a woman wait for a man to take her away?

42

It's the season when the storks fly by.

Beyond the last hill, the last house, there are wheat fields, and in these wheat fields, if you know how to approach them without frightening them, you can see the storks, placid.

I don't kill storks, nor do I kill swallows. They are sacred birds, my mother told me, like the grebe and the turtledove, it's written in the place that says she must say her prayers at a set time.

When the first storks arrived, the spotters—I was one of

them—ran toward the village yelling, "the storks, the storks" as if a miracle had just occurred.

43

They say that I am Righteous. A killer, can he be Righteous?

44

There is chaos.

45

Kill the creators of chaos. But kill them all. So not a one survives. I'm told that a firearm would be preferable. I'm told this gently.

46

The woman left the blue house. I don't read the messages that she sends a boy to bring me. The child waits for a moment but understands that I have nothing to give him for her. He seems like a good messenger. The papers accumulate on the small table where I throw them. I'll have to burn them.

I saw her in town with a powerful man for whom greed has no limits. I know also that his cruelty, of which evidence has accumulated, is tolerated. He is feared as if he possessed an occult power.

He is next on the list. The first Councilman of the Supreme Leader.

47

They starve the body and the soul, but they binge in the secret rooms of the blue house, fond of the young, very young virgins that they make bleed. The cries of the bleeding beasts are louder than screeching violins in an orchestra. Women dance, women sing, young men serve drinks, business is good. Images are passed around that wake them up from their blissful drowsiness, and they begin their feast again, with new flesh, golden grapes, scarlet pomegranates, poppies gathered at dawn, whiskey and cocaine.

I saw them. I was not hidden, I was serving, a servant among the servants trained for their tasks in the house, hidden even among the experts who have been working for a long time. Practiced in service and in silence. The one who spoke outdoors was later found in the garbage, victim of a street accident.

At the end of the night, they continue to chat. To scribes they dictate the text of the next speech that will pronounce the good of all the people. They say that business is good. They prosper in the chaos and ruin.

48

Did God allow killing in his name?

God, and him alone, can strike. In his name.

The man who kills is a criminal, simple as that. A miserable assassin.

God curses murderers.

God did not reach this land.

I am cursed, and they still say that I am Righteous.

49

I saw the woman again with the first Councilman of the Palace. They were walking with impunity. He kisses her with a full mouth on the leather seats in the back of the Rolls. I see trickles of drool through the windowpane.

I've known the chauffeur since childhood, his father was cut loose as an employee; he lent me the Rolls. I drove around like a leader, without a servant hat, up to a famous spring in the Plateaus. I filled ten bottles to drink and to water the curly red carnations. I saved one bottle for my friend.

How long ago did he leave town? I don't know anymore. He doesn't write me, and I don't write him. He doesn't miss me, for me it's like he never left. He said he would return; he'll return. I don't wait around for him, I will know when. He's like a twin brother to me, he's the first one that I met in the town, I didn't know anyone. He writes books that I don't read. He tells me nothing about himself, I tell him nothing about myself, each knows everything about the other, that's the way it is.

He could have been my enemy; he's my friend.

50

The Councilman that I saw drooling and kissing the woman owns a horse-breeding farm to the east of the village where I was born. It's the most famous stud farm in the region. The purebreds are sent to equestrian training centers.

Armed guards protect the estate, in uniform they circulate the grounds in a Jeep, dogs accompany them.

I'll go down there.

51

He was galloping on an English mare. At dawn, the mare hit a sharp rock in the middle of the path. I grabbed the unbalanced man, I laid him out on the ground. He didn't struggle.

The sun was rising. He must have seen the shining blade. He was not afraid, he didn't say anything, he didn't try to talk to me or buy me off, he closed his eyes.

I spared the horse.

52

Between two pots of red carnations by my window, I found a message. I had just returned from the Plateaus, where I had stayed several days, far from my mother's house.

The woman begs me to help her find her lover's murderer. I think about the hours I spent with her, her soft white skin, her timid voice—she sometimes sang ancient songs I recognized but didn't know. I don't know where she is from.

She said she loves me. Did I believe her?

53

How to believe a woman? Women and their ruses . . .

I would have liked to meet the prince, the one who searches for the science of women and love. Obeying the king, his father, he traveled far and long to meet women, to get to know them, their beauty and ugliness, vices and virtues, and then to choose the most beautiful one, the most successful, the finest, she who would become the prince's spouse, the mother to little princes and princesses. My grandmother told me these legends in secret, my mother didn't approve of it. My maternal grandmother used to tell me while laughing, "You are my prince. I have a princess for you, you won't have to deal with traveling or meeting random women."

She died when I was still a child.

I didn't find the prince and the women . . . The one I loved, the only one, maybe the woman that my grandmother intended for me, she disappeared one day, I looked for her and then I stopped looking.

54

I was given a sophisticated silencer. I didn't refuse it. I'll keep it, it's a collectible item.

As for me, I prefer the knife or the razor.

55

In a working-class cabaret I go to regularly to listen to an unknown singer who had been taken on by the boss a few months ago, and who sang for the nuptials of a wealthy lover, I thought I recognized the man. A man who was still young, tall, handsome. He was alone.

I returned, less for the singer than for him. He was there. Still alone, without bodyguards. I thought I was mistaken. He's the man of the Secret. How many of the missing were given up to the vultures in the nearby mountain?

It's said that he fell in love with the singer. Madly in love. He comes, he listens, he leaves. He speaks to nobody, nobody speaks to him.

It's a poor cabaret for the poor. Who would believe that this humble and silent man was all-powerful?

I like the singer.

56

The Citadel was built in a prohibited area. Many nearby villages had to be evacuated to construct the battlements and watchmen's towers that surround it. The Plateaus are controlled from the hills. The Citadel, with its murderers, high walls, and patrol paths, is inaccessible. Those who work inside it don't leave, they live as if they were inside a town.

The Supreme Leader had his mausoleum constructed in a thicket of odorous trees near a fountain, he entrusted his plans to a famous architect.

My father, lying under the tree, barefoot.

The soldiers didn't see the rats at night. They keep their distance from the body, standing along the low wall that separates the courtyard from the first house, because of the smell. The head officer that appointed the guards had made clear that the odor had to infest the entire town and the surrounding fields, reaching the next hamlet, so as to make an example.

My mother refused to acknowledge the odor of the rotting cadaver, she said, "I recognize the scent of your father, the sweating leather, the mare's fur, the fragrant plants, the powder indicating his return from hunting, the smell of the Plateaus—that is your father. Who says all that smells bad? Those people lie, may they be cursed . . . The brass bed has kept the odor of the brute. I loved him, I love him, he cannot stink. They threw a dead badger in the square, that's why they talk of a pestilent odor. He was the pure air, the stormy wind, the crazy gallop, the warm hands that caressed the behind of a woman . . . He's not dead. He's not lying under the tree. He's walking the Plateaus at dusk on his white mare, he's walking and he's meditating." My mother talked, my mother talked too much. I thought she was going insane. She talked for so long, people listened or didn't, then she no longer talked.

When I left, she didn't say anything. She didn't know why I was leaving the house never to return, she'll never know. I'm older now. I leaned in toward her, she took me by the elbow, her small hand drew me toward her, she kissed me on the forehead like a son leaving for far away, for a long time. She gave me her blessing. I left.

Did my mother know what people were saying? People talked a lot about my father, about his cruelty. I heard stories that my mother could not believe. Nothing was said to my face, but I learned to listen without being present. From one incident to another, men who talked among themselves, what had they actually seen? I never knew. I listened, terrified, I was still not yet a man. My father, was it my father? I listened. The men said that if he hadn't died he would've terrorized the region and maybe all the land. They added that he died like a fighting tiger, not weakening until he received the hit that finished him.

I also no longer saw the rats under the tree.

58

I wanted to hear the singer's voice. The boss claims that she's an orphan he took in. Girls like her disappear every day. Families post notices in the papers, all in vain.

She sings every evening. The boss barely pays her. She is housed, fed. She's not from the town. I went to the cabaret. The woman no longer comes. Apparently the man sent her to the Citadel. Life down there is austere. The voice of a young girl, amplified by the arches around the courtyards planted with box trees and pomegranate trees . . . He bought the boss's silence. Who doesn't know that the orphan is locked in the Citadel?

59

The master of ceremonies organizes a falcon hunt. The Citadel feels like it has been besieged by armed men.

60

The Citadel of the Plateaus is fortified, forbidden. How could I hear the young girl's voice from so far away? I was downwind, but the walls are tall. Was she put in the watchman's tower? Is she locked up in a secret tower? It was her voice, I'm sure of it. We were walking with the shepherd, the son of my father's shepherd, a dynasty known throughout the entire region. He still tries to teach me how to ride a horse, he is patient, we're the same age.

Like me, at the same time, he stopped to listen. What I say is true. He looked at me. He said to me, "You don't love her, I hope? She is his, he's jealous, she sings for him. The others, his guests, hear only her voice, he doesn't show her. You won't see her again. If she displeases him one day . . . But she is very young. Don't wait. She's a prisoner, and might be happy. Don't wait. Forget her, forget her . . ."

He repeated several times the advice that I did not follow. I didn't respond, I didn't talk about the girl. I only listened to the song, and he listened as well.

We walked for a long time. I know now what I need to

know. I know what happens in the hidden districts of the Citadel. It's also a disciplinary citadel.

The falconry hunt will be princely.

61

I went hunting with the shepherd's son using a bow and arrow.

I injured a young falcon and I was about to finish it with my knife, like I used to do with the birds that we brought back in our bags.

My mother used to lament over the beheaded spoils that I threw onto the green kitchen tiles in the same manner that my father threw them. "My son, my son, why the massacre? Birds . . . You mistake birds for tigers. The father of your grandfather hunted the tiger and the lion. That's what is said—he was never afraid, he was always the first to attack the wild beasts . . . I threw an old tiger skin with the head, the leather had holes like a mosquito net . . ." My mother dreaded these returns from hunting with bow and arrow, I always returned agitated and talkative. She didn't like to hear about our exploits, and my skill didn't impress her.

The shepherd's son took the young falcon in his hands, he forbade me from touching it. He would take it home and care for it, and once it healed he would train it how he had learned. It was my falcon, my arrow had injured it, it belonged to me. Despite my companion's calm patience that protected the bird from my desire, we fought until we drew blood. The bird was lying on the ground, we were too. I was the first to get back up, I took the bird that was still alive, I saw my enemy's alarmed eyes, I didn't kill the falcon, I placed it in the palms of his trembling hands.

After that day, we no longer went hunting together.

The son of my father's shepherd is the owner of the stud farm, the primary organizer of the falconry hunts. The master of the Citadel, the Cursed One, had demanded the most beautiful horses, the best falcons, the most skillful falconers. The great quartermaster is at his service. The master loves his cabaret singers, horses, and falcons. He prefers the Citadel of the Plateaus over his city palace.

The master of the hunt who taught me how to shoot a bow and arrow knows the Citadel. I spoke to him about the tower that's too high for a kidnapping. I know that the lover no longer takes out the beloved woman, I know it, I also live in a world where . . .

I will kidnap the singer.

62

I saw the man at the stud farm. He has a long straight neck, tanned from all of the horse training.

He is handsome.

63

From the screeching of the birds that were flying in disarray a few dozen meters from me, I knew there would be water. There was water, I verified its presence each time, and when I told my mother the miracle of the water in the desert

Plateaus she said, "You see, the Book tells the truth, it always tells the truth, don't forget it." I didn't forget my mother's words, but I learned that the Book can lie.

I asked my mother to read me the same story again and again, I looked at the letters in the book without understanding them, she protested but she read it anyway. I loved my mother's voice, vibrant and warm, while she reread the story of Abraham and his son. Her voice suddenly became somber, she paused silently for a moment before beginning to read. "She went on her way and wandered in the Desert of Beersheba."

When I told her later that I had seen the bush and the well, my mother began to laugh: "The desert of the Plateaus is not the desert of Hagar and Ishmael . . . Abraham chased Hagar away from her house with her young son. He gave them bread and a goatskin full of water, and he chased them out, he knew the desert would kill them. Sarah wanted the deaths of Hagar and Ishmael, she loved Isaac, her son, and she hated Hagar and Ishmael, the son of Abraham and Hagar. She ordered Abraham to chase out her servant, Ishmael's mother; Ishmael would not be the heir of Abraham, his father. Hagar obeyed. She was a slave, an Egyptian princess reduced to the status of a slave, plundered in war . . . even though she had given Abraham a son and had shared her bed with him under the orders of old Sarah. Hagar was not the legitimate spouse. They were alone in the desert, without bread, without water, Ishmael was going to die. 'I pray that I don't see my child die,' Hagar repeated while crying. She threw him into a bush . . ."

My mother would always interrupt the story here and say, "What could she do, the miserable woman? What could she do, alone, abandoned in the murderous desert?" She added, "I would have given him my heart to eat. My heart, yes. And if he did not have teeth yet he would have sucked the blood, he would not be dead . . . Yes, my heart."

I listened to my mother, I said nothing, I believed her. She continued, "Hagar heard a voice that told her to bring her son to the well. The angel opened Hagar's eyes and she saw a water well. Ishmael grew up in the desert with his mother Hagar who didn't leave him until her death. He became the most skilled archer in the land."

After reading the same passage several time, my mother decided to stop. I waited anyway, with my eyes closed, but my mother was quiet. She didn't leave the room. I said to her, "Abraham didn't love his sons . . . He loved God before his sons."

My mother looked at me, attentive, uneasy, "He loved God and his sons."

I persisted, "He didn't love his sons, he sacrificed them."

My mother hastily responded, "But they didn't die. If Abraham hadn't loved God from the beginning, his sons would be dead."

I was quiet for a moment, then said firmly, "No. Abraham wanted to kill his sons, he didn't love them. Neither Isaac nor Ishmael." Again I became quiet, my mother didn't interrupt my silence. I said, "And Sarah, Isaac's mother, and Hagar, Ishmael's mother . . . They left Abraham alone . . . They didn't say anything? He was their son, all the same, he was their only son . . ." I was going to cry, I didn't want to cry.

My mother took me in her arms, I smelled my mother's scent of the young fruits that she cared for at dawn, every morning, and she said to me, "My gazelle, my little falcon, Sarah and Hagar were unaware of all of Abraham's actions, of the sacrifice his God demanded of him, it was a secret between God and him."

"What do you think Sarah and Hagar would have done if they had known?"

My mother dried my tears with her warm, soft hands. "My gazelle, don't cry. Sarah and Hagar would have protected their child with their life, Abraham would have had to fight their body to reach the child . . . God wouldn't have allowed the murder of a mother. Believe me. I'm telling you the truth." My mother held me in her arms, she sang an old lullaby, I fell asleep.

Later, in my mother's old trunk, I looked for the book that she would read to me every time I asked her to. I didn't find it.

64

The singer disappeared. I didn't kidnap her.

The falcon hunt didn't take place.

There is talk of an imminent catastrophe. What catastrophe, when there's already chaos?

I thought I had lost my razor with the horned handle.

65

During an orgy in a secret room in the Citadel, in the middle of the painted women, the nude dancers, the singers covered in gold, and the black horses decorated like sacrificial rams, the master of the Citadel, the man of the Secret, committed suicide.

The blood flowed for a long time.

Men and women deserted the room. Only the screeching horses and falcons remained.

66

The only object from my mother's house that I keep in my room is the cedar trunk she gave me. I hid the razor in it among the books. My room is a cell. A bed, a table, a chair, my mother's trunk at the edge of the window with the red carnations, a sink in a corner, and above it a folding mirror so I can shave. I regularly go to the municipal showers, there are no baths in the neighborhood.

67

I looked for the singer in the large town.

68

I returned to the slaughterhouses. I enjoy this walk. I cross the town on foot from the highest hill to the road beyond the populated areas, sometimes I stop at the square with the blooming pomegranate trees in the neglected Jardin d'Essai. The trees still grow, vigorously flowering. In my mother's house there was a pomegranate tree, she said it was a hundred years old, she protected it from my pocketknife, the wood of the pomegranate tree makes the best slingshots . . . I don't know any other flowers with the same precious red color, maybe the poppy, a red that overwhelms me. This is the color of the fleshy mouths of little girls, the violent lips of courtesans, and the velour dress that I once gave a woman. It was a slim dress for her slim body, made with a velour of the same red as a pomegranate flower . . . I asked her to never take it off, not during the day or at night, for as long as the red remained red. She obeyed me for seven days and seven nights, until the morning where she tore the dress right under my eyes with the tip of a thin kitchen knife, I let her do it and then I chased her out, I didn't see her again.

In the slaughterhouses I know a high priest who worked with my father when they were young. He gives me his long knife, sharp like Suleiman's saber, and I take his place. We don't speak.

69

I put a carnation in the buttonhole of my jacket and left my room at dawn.

70

Is God really God in forgiving a murderer?

71

I've cut the throats of Barbarians. I'm not a killer. I sacrifice for Liberty, Justice, Truth, for my People, even if they ask nothing of me. It's my mission, I don't talk about it, I would be taken for a madman.

I will cut the throats of other Barbarians.

Are we not in a state of Barbarism?

72

They don't have a praetorian guard like the high dignitaries, they're more secretive, the clandestine nature protects them better than the men of the State.

I work alone. I don't have an accomplice during the hunt.

My only friend was assassinated.

I followed him, from the hills of the olive trees to the sepulcher in the cemetery of his birth village.

There were three that murdered the poet, my friend.

73

The singer has disappeared.

74

In exchange for a piece of gold I stole from my mother, the black servant opened for me the door to the forbidden room.

My mother's grandfather and father both died before I reached the age at which one of them could let me enter the locked room. They didn't hand down the épée to me, nor the Ancestral sword, nor the dagger, nor the saber.

Since their absence, nobody has entered this room. My mother didn't want to answer my questions. She said that if God had summoned her father and grandfather so early, then he had a reason, hidden from her, that prevented her from opening for me the door to which she had the key.

I looked for the key. In vain. How did the black servant thieve it from my mother? When he drew the thick red curtain, the harsh light lit up the walls. To me it looked like beams of gold and silver. Ancient white weapons, strangely decorated, exposed in a room too small for their radiance.

I begged the servant to accompany me at night with a torch.

75

I looked for a long time.

There are three of them. They act together.

Who would expect the transvestite cabarets and back rooms where pornographic films are continuously playing?

I have my caves, they have theirs.

76

I walk through the town like I walked on the stone ground, for a long time, not tiring, I don't stop but I watch, I have the eye of a vulture. I'm outside the town when I realize the distance I've traveled, I had been walking aimlessly, I stop.

I walked very far. I crossed the villages all the way to the wastelands sprinkled with abandoned greenhouses, except for one, hidden by the wild grass. I noticed silhouettes, undoubtedly farm hands, I approached, the human forms disappeared. There were lines of tomato plants, and at the back there was a kind of tool shed made out of reeds.

I pushed the door open, somebody let out a yell. A woman. She was not alone. I thought of my mother's tales about the women who are raped during war, soft spoils, almost always young women, very young, and about the children in their bellies, detested newborns that witches are contracted to do away with.

These children are bastards, planted in the women's bellies by the enemy so that they can continue to rob the descendants with their blood. It is not enough to kill the men and confiscate their land. They need to take the women's bodies, force them like virgins, possess them in pleasure and in pain; spoils of war, pleasures of love. The children who are not killed are sometimes found fighting as mercenaries in a war that isn't theirs.

Night began to fall, I could no longer see anything. I returned to the red dirt path, I sat down on a rock not far from the greenhouse, I waited.

I recognized the voice before I recognized the song. It was the voice from the tower, the voice from the cabaret. I stood up, I was not mistaken, she was singing, for whom?

She is alive.

77

It seems that he's so afraid that he disguises himself as a woman when he's not in his bunker. He's a high-ranking officer, I know that he tortures people.

78

I returned to the place with the greenhouse where I heard the woman singing. The reed shed was empty and in ruin.

I wandered around the town. I went to every place where she might sing. I know the private residences where the master invites singers and musicians for the night, from the shabbiest to the most refined houses. I went everywhere.

79

The confusion is that one killer is just as good as another.

80

Where to find a man who disguises himself as a woman?

81

My mother waited for me late into the night. I returned from the Plateaus, from our dangerous errands, almost always alone, my mother wasn't asleep. She listened under the giant fig tree in the interior courtyard by the light of the gas lamp that she hung on the lowest branch. Near her, asleep on a fine wool carpet, lies the young black girl. I knew that my mother didn't lift her eyes from the page she pretended to be reading. I walked toward her, I kissed her on the forehead, we didn't speak.

I remember the night when I returned holding a live eagle in a net, he was bleeding.

My mother stood up slowly, she placed her book at the foot of the fig tree, she didn't cry out. She moved toward me and said, "The eagle is beautiful, and you are courageous. You didn't kill it, that's good. You fought with it and you won. It's night, but I will accompany you to the village to make sure that you free it. Your father's not here, I'm in charge. Don't run away, wait for me."

Beyond the last grave in the cemetery, the eagle flew away, it disappeared into the night. I obeyed my mother while crying.

82

I didn't find the injured eagle the next day nor in the following days, I didn't succeed in catching another one, despite my tenacity and despite the excellent arrows that I cut with my grandfather's old pocketknife, which he gave me before his death.

On horseback, like my father, I would have been much faster.

I see a man galloping alone on the Plateaus at dawn. He pursues a gazelle or a deer, I'm crouched behind a rock, he's far away; guided by his master, the beast makes twists and turns that stimulate the stealth and the grace of the animal. I hear several gunshots that get progressively closer. Standing, I can see the hunt, the galloping and the jumping, until the beast becomes exhausted.

One morning, before the smell of coffee had permeated the house, my father woke up my mother with the whimpers of a young gazelle. The first gift of the morning from my father to my mother was an injured gazelle. "She's for you, I don't want to kill her, you will treat her, she will be your companion." My mother treated the gazelle, her gazelle, loyal and tender, until the day a watchdog ripped its throat; it had ventured outside of the walls, it had to be put down. My father promised my mother the next young gazelle.

The hunter wouldn't kill the gazelle, he would succeed in catching it alive and he would give it to my mother. I waited. After the last gunshot, the gazelle fell to the ground. The man dismounted his horse. I ran toward him, he couldn't see me.

He would turn around, I would run into his arms, he would lift me up while laughing, he would lift me very high, and he would have me sit astride his stallion, he would gallop, I would be pressed against him, the gazelle would still be alive in the bag.

The hunter was not my father, the gazelle was no longer breathing.

Maybe my mother would have refused another young gazelle.

83

Every time I strike, I am invisible. I am the Angel that whispers into the ear, near the throat, I whisper the last words that can't be written down, the incredible words, unique to the precise second where the knife cuts life short.

The Angel's voice pulsates like fresh blood.

84

The first one fell under the bougainvillea vines that cover an old wall parallel to the sidewalk. He was armed.

The second, in front of the small deserted screen on which a pornographic film was playing. He was armed.

The third, in a back alley; his body slipped on the greasy cobblestones. He was armed.

The Angel didn't speak a single word.

There were three of them. They killed my only friend, the poet. They are dead now. I murdered them.

85

The beekeeper's honey, golden and gooey, is better than the honey from the Plateaus, it should be licked off of a woman's skin, it's a honey for Princes. The Plateau honey is wild, rough, I loved it, I don't eat it anymore.

86

I don't watch television, I don't listen to the radio, I don't read the papers.

I know everything.

It's enough to walk through the town.

87

I'm told that she sings for weddings.

88

Did I invent the woman who sang in the shed at the other end of the vandalized greenhouses? Nothing remains of the beautiful gardens and the orchards—nothing. The town with its slums becomes progressively more disorganized and miserable, it's a harmful ogre, it devours the farmland. Where are the orange trees? The farmland, once fertile, now neglected. The singer's voice, did I believe I heard her? Hallucinations. Am I crazy? That day I had smoked neither hashish nor opium. The shed disappeared.

Inside the disused greenhouse, nothing is visible except for uncovered iron arches and a few scraps of transparent plastic. The reed shed existed, I'm sure of it, I heard a woman singing. Then the shed was destroyed, that very shed, the shed at the edge of the field that lays fallow. I walked almost to the spot where I heard her voice, nothing remains, not a single reed. And her?

I'm not making anything up, I'm not spreading rumors, but I believe in the rumor, it helps me understand the town, and I am not mistaken. The clandestine greenhouse was first destroyed, now it has disappeared, I'm sure that it existed and I saw it with my eyes, I could have touched it if the voice had not prevented me from doing so. The rumor will guide me to kill he who disguises himself as a woman, I know it. The rumor says nothing of the singer that I didn't kidnap from the Citadel tower.

I had things to do. I didn't know then that the man would kill himself. I wait for her to return, she went to sing beyond the border, I am patient.

This woman is not imaginary.

89

During the days of blood, the woman refused to see men. She was not locked away; instead she locked her own door, a voluntary prisoner in the room, but she was not alone. On the sofa covered in small red carnations, other women of the house joined her in these peaceful days in which the lute and their voices could be heard beyond the nearby woods and the garden cedars, from the pale-green tiles supporting the women's bodies.

I entered the room at midday. She was lying on the carnations as if struck with a fatal illness.

She had lied to me. I abandoned her.

I don't go out anymore. How long has it been since I left my room? On the window ledge somebody leaves honey, coffee, and bread. Messages are slid under the door, I don't read them.

They're getting impatient. I don't work for them. I am free.

The one who disguises himself as a woman is still alive. I'm sure that they're threatening me. I do not fear death. Them, yes.

I know what they won't know.

I knew, by the way the message reached me, that I would open it and it would tell me what I want to know.

I read it.

It's a trap.

My mother. She was still young and beautiful. My father loved her. That was before the massacre.

He left. My mother knew nothing of his hunts, of his

travels to lands near and far, of his nights in the throes of love. Did she only know that the men, poets, merchants and musicians, smokers of hashish and opium, would find themselves in secret rooms where women sang choruses that they themselves had composed, accompanied by a lute or a lyre, and that night after night, for seven nights, the women recited and danced; did these women offer the paradises of their bodies and their voices to these men? In this way, until dawn, there was amorous, poetic, and musical jousting. When day arrived, the wise and clever women left the sleeping men; these men's wives would not see them before the eighth day.

My mother didn't ask my father any questions. He was there. He would return for her, he told her, and she believed him. He said that she was the only woman capable of holding on to him. Of course he left, but he knew that when he returned the bathroom would be warm and the water would be plentiful . . . The bath tiles were ready for the rejuvenation of his body and spirit. My mother sensed the moment when she herself had to prepare the room for the ritual bath that would return her husband to her. The perfumes, the ointments, the fine towels, the embroidered clothing, fresh fruit in a bowl shaped like a lion's head, she forgot nothing.

I heard the servants whispering. Women and men do not meet at the baths, husbands do not lock themselves away with their wives, but my father invited my mother to enter the steam room. Hidden behind the columns, the servants watched for the moment when my mother silently pushed open the door to the bath, they detected her vague smile, her rosier cheeks. They had prepared tea, cakes, and other sweets for the master. My mother sat on the silk cushions, with her legs crossed, she took an old book from the cedar trunk, she had picked the sweetest, most beautiful figs, the kind that I prefer, round and violet.

My mother, alone with my father. The singing voice reads poems that I don't understand, I'm still young. My father listens, the narghile whistles, the white dove walks on the brown wooden railing in silence. My mother's laugh.

The servants leave the couple's room, but they see everything, they know everything, and they talk. I am also eagerly waiting; I listen to the most talkative servants. They say that my father bites the fleshy fig the way a man bites a woman's breast. They say that he laughs while offering my mother the other red half, moist from his saliva. They say that my mother opens her soft, lovely mouth toward the fig that my father slips onto her red tongue. They say that my father tells my mother a story of blood, of figs, and of women, in a low voice the servants say a word I misunderstand, the gesture that accompanies this word moves from the heart to the top of the thigh, right where the flowers are on the servants' dresses. They laugh, they repeat the action until the last fig is eaten. They say, "He's the falcon, she's the fig." And they laugh.

Me, I don't laugh.

93

Will I have to cross oceans and continents more barbaric than my own?

He would have been removed and thrown to the crocodiles, into a lion's den or in a cell under an electronic eye.

She's in the house next door, and I don't know?

94

The man disguised as a woman was very afraid when I approached him . . . The cabaret was dark due to an electrical failure.

A poor man under a poor woman. He had given the order to kill a long time ago. He's the one who attends the executions, it's known that he enjoys them. I'm not talking about the legal executions decreed by law, those are less numerous. He does what he wants, he is feared.

In the candlelight, the faces were difficult to distinguish. I was very near the man. He removed his wig, the pearl necklace scattered under the velour bench dyed red with oxblood. He didn't cry out, he slid gently under the table like a dead drunk client.

I walk through the streets of the town. I drink a coffee at the counter among the noise of beer drinkers, young and old, idle, swaggering and talkative, they no longer hide themselves in order to drink, they wait for death, they won't try to defend themselves.

People speak to me, I don't respond.

There is a woman at her window. I hear her singing. The house isn't a brothel. I approach the voice under the cracked balcony, one day it will collapse, the woman will continue her song in the ruins, we live in rubble. I barely see the woman, she hangs her laundry on the iron wires that extend past the balcony. She sings, she is a housekeeper among the rusting wires and the young children's clothes. She is young and ugly. I stopped. She doesn't see me, leaning against a tree trunk, there are still a few whitewashed tree branches. I listen to her. Did the singer disguise herself as a young spouse, a family woman, a housewife? Did she become ugly out of loyalty? The voice moved away, lost to a dark room where I perceive nothing.

Today the Angel doesn't accompany me. I go very quickly among the graves of the cemetery on the hill. The ancient stones no longer have any markings, at the foot of the trees neither numbers nor letters are legible on the unearthed funeral stones. Women squatting in a circle around a grave are talking and praying. The cemetery covers the hill, it's as old as the town itself, the first of this wretched continent.

I walked to the mausoleum that the victor of the revolt, my father's assassin, ordered to be constructed—with what money? The mausoleum will be a palace with funeral chambers and anterooms, musicians will play pieces commissioned from the most famous composers all night and day, renowned artists will paint frescoes inspired by and glorifying the beloved victor, giant sculptures will stand watch in the corner of each outer wall, they will be the guardians of death. Guards, who will be the most attractive men, dressed by famous couturiers, will endlessly patrol the length of the outer high wall of the empty fortress where the embalmed body will lie, watched over the sophisticated machines that will prevent it from rotting like a human corpse. He had calculated everything with architects and scientists, everything was planned.

On the marble platform a flower garden had been set up where the bodily remains will be exposed in a casket of refrigerated glass. The entire town, including even the little children, will bow down at the foot of the catafalque before joining the procession that will accompany him to his birth village. On the pathway to his ancestral home he will be cheered, praised, and mourned.

Young virgins crowned with orange blossoms and beautiful young men chosen from princely families will follow the casket in front of the family. The family will be followed by the praetorian guard on horseback, high dignitaries, the general staff in full dress uniform—the secretive Services won't show themselves—then the favored artists will go, the musicians who won't stop playing until reaching the birth house, the poets who will recite verses written for him, the official painters and sculptors, actors in performance attire—he loved theater. The people from the deserts and the mountains will follow at the end, hurrying to the sea to pay their respects.

The funerals for the Supreme Leader will be grandiose, with his portrait on banners, billboards, everywhere. The people will wear mourning dress for an entire year, the design for the women's and the men's clothing had already been created, and he also commissioned the design of the uniform of those who will oversee the precise implementation of the regulations for national mourning.

The victor of the revolt, the Supreme Leader, doesn't know what I know, nor do the others. I will obey only myself. At the bottom of the ravine where his car will have slid, in the dust and the thorns, he will be killed, the ground studded with oleanders will drink up the very last criminal drop of blood. The abandoned mausoleum will be pillaged stone by stone, fragments of the painted walls will be sold at the cemetery entrance, the hollow statues will be destroyed by the slingshots of boys living on the streets, the fine wood sculptures will be snatched from the balustrades and from the platforms to be burned; during the winter, in metal and cardboard shacks, the mosaic tiles and the lapis lazuli will decorate the graves of the poor flanking the hill.

He died at twilight, his bloodless body is laid under the red laurel flowers. I hear vultures.

They circle the corpse of the Supreme Leader.

96

They'll be ruthless, I know them. They think I'm the assassin.

I didn't kill him.

I'm the only son. The first. The Only One. "A gift from God," said the young and old servants. My mother, young, suddenly sterile? My father has had daughters and sons, I learned, rumor says all, the land is vast, my father crossed it on horseback, he made children at each stopping place, I don't know them, could my father count and name them all? Servants from far away came and told strange stories among themselves, I was young, they let me sleep between their thighs, tightly pressed around the large wooden plates where they kneaded pastry dough for a secret party. I hear them, they speak a language that mixes words from the Plateaus with words from the sea, I don't understand everything they say. Why does my father's name race from one mouth to the other? I discover my father among the softness of the shore and the bitterness of the wormwood tangles, among the oleander and the acacia, they speak too quickly, I didn't have to pretend to be asleep to follow those high and low pitches, but if I straightened up and looked at them they stopped talking. In this manner, the fraternal network of my father's meandering journeys takes shape. My mother doesn't want to know anything about her husband's happy wanderings, she doesn't listen to the servants' bitter words, eventually they leave her alone and stop whispering about the loyalty of their overly loving mistress.

They're preparing a party for me.

On the Plateaus, from the ridge where I walk alone, I see in the distance, on the dirt path, the black musicians; they crawl like drunkards and only play beyond the outermost village walls. I'm looking for the lion. My mother's father told me that a tall old black slave walked through the streets of the village every year. A black musician who played the drums and kept a lion on a leash. He stopped in front of certain houses, he must have known which households had the most children. He didn't enter, he waited for the doorway to creak open, the servant informed her mistress who would come with her sons, then, one by one, the black man would place them on the lion's back to guarantee them a long life. He earned a few coins this way, some food, and then he continued his travels from village to village. My grandmother added that, every time, at least three sons who had ridden the savage beast died during the year; this made her laugh, I don't know why. I asked her if my father, her firstborn son, had ever mounted the lion's back, she answered that he had been the first from the village and even the region to rise to the challenge, because at that time the lion was still young. The lion must have died, and the black man didn't replace him. Maybe he died during his journeys? Apparently he later went around with a giraffe. My grandmother has seen the giraffe. The sultans and the European princes demanded giraffes, cheetahs, tigers, and leopards from far away for their royal menageries.

I often imagined the giraffes' voyage by boat, from Africa to an overseas land and a "City of Light"; that's how my father called it when he told the story in my mother's house after returning from a long month of absence, the enchanting land, rivers, streams, the fertile landscapes . . . The inhabitants came along the roads and paths, the farmers abandoned their animals and fields to admire the procession: my father with his followers, on horseback, the prince of the steppes, turbans with golden thread, burnooses of fine wool, he must have looked like the Emir. My mother asked him, "Will you take me there?" He promised his sweetheart he would. My mother has never left the grand house, the beautiful house of her master, my father. Until that wretched day when they assassinated my father, when my mother became a poor madwoman.

I run toward the house to announce the musicians' arrival. I'm seven years old. Before reaching our door, a heavy oak door studded with gilded copper, I hear the sheep that my father gave me and that I raised. The black butcher is pulling him, the sheep doesn't want to walk. The sheep is decorated with red and green woolen pom-poms around his head and his neck. Who adorned him that way? My mother hid me on the day of the sacrifice. She confided my sheep to the youngest servant who didn't tell me anything. I approached the black man and fought him with my fists. He let me hit him, he said, "Your father ordered it." I calmed down. On my right ankle I was wearing the magical charm fashioned by my mother's servants, my father didn't see the blue magician's cloth, he would've hit my mother and her servants. I didn't see him wipe his face and eyes with the bleeding sheep skin like the men do, the fathers who protect their families against misfortune and illness. People say that in the Occident, a tradition taken from the Orient, women stain white wool with virgin blood from their wedding night and pass it across their eyes; in this way they preserve the lively eye of youth. I cried, alone, squatting on the house doorstep, the black man disappeared at the end of the road, pulling the recalcitrant sheep. For the last time I cried.

I saw the blood from the sacrifice. Not the blade thrust into the beast's throat. I saw the blood from the celebration, I didn't cry, the knife didn't scare me. I thought about my mother's words, "Abraham didn't kill his son, he honored God . . . Abraham didn't kill his son, he loved God."

I didn't eat the white kidneys. The female servants prepared them for me, they say that only men eat these organs from the sacrificed beast, and that they guarantee masculinity. But I know that these women also savored them in secret, laughing among themselves at the idea of a metamorphosis; but some of the women had already eaten so many of them, without any noticeable change, that the youngest servants amused themselves and teased each other with their mouths full of white kidneys, golden, sour, delicious.

My mother, young and sterile after her first son, was loved by my father as both spouse and courtesan.

It was the Angel that informed me. He had just learned of the murder of the Supreme Leader, that bloodthirsty victor of the revolt. I felt the Angel standing across from me at the window while for one last time I watered the curly red Sweet Williams, growing in tight clumps, hardy plants; they were dying when I first arrived in this room that I'm now leaving because they're looking for me.

The Angel accompanies me. He will disappear when I find the singer. He doesn't help me, maybe he thinks that she works for the secret Police force or terrorist groups. He doesn't say anything, I don't know anything.

If the body were embalmed, it would have been placed during the service at the heart of the elegant Mausoleum, in the golden radiance, while trumpets played the eulogy. After the national funerals, some people met up in the mausoleums for clandestine pleasure. They didn't realize that the armed guards wouldn't have stopped the crowd, retracing its steps after the senior figures departed, from desecrating the tyrant's tomb.

If the corpse were exhumed, it would have been undressed; stripped bare; beaten; insulted; stained with slimy, tubercular, bloody spit; it would have been dragged by the hair, real or fake, to the foot of the tree for the ravens to peck at; it would have been chopped up, and the atrophied penis and testicles would have been stuffed into his mouth; the pieces of flesh would have been abandoned to the vultures, and the burning of the mausoleum would have been sublime among the radiant gilded gold, the cobalt blue and the lime green of the ceramic pieces decorated with little red carnations.

I am not afraid of death.

Under the ring's smooth, flat coral stone, I concealed the

hemlock from the Plateaus. The son of my father's shepherd, the one who guards his flock of sheep day and night, he's the one who taught me about stones, rocks, bushes and secret caves, wormwood, sagebrush, acacia. He's also the one who confided me the secret under oath, I swore never to reveal it, I kept my promise, he had me gather the poison among the medicinal plants. Women in black walk along the Plateaus, old madwomen followed by the shepherd's son; he knew that they would lead him to the place where nobody would have dared to venture. In the hollow of a rock, hidden under small stones, that was where he first found the unknown plant that kills. I gave him old pieces of gold that my grandmother had been saving for her granddaughters when they married. But instead she gave them to me, the only son of her eldest child, she gave the gold pieces to me, but not all of them, I don't know where she's hiding the others, I looked for them, I looked under paving stones and tiling, I found nothing.

I know that they'll bleed me out like the big black man bled out the sacrificial sheep.

I will not be tortured with small slits of the blade in an underground dungeon or in a shepherd's shed surrounded by barbed wire. Like the Angel, but more faithful, the beneficial plant accompanies me, it will save me from the barbarism of my brothers.

I don't track them anymore, I'm the one being tracked. I don't hide.

I went back to see the beekeeper.

I walked from hill to hill, caressing the deadly stone in my ring. I keep the horn handle of my father's razor secure in my jacket pocket. The coral and the horn are my talismans.

I hear singing coming from the path that leads to the beehive. Maybe a voice that doesn't exist, a voice within me, or even the voice of the invisible Angel that laughs. Yesterday the reed shed at the back of the greenhouse, the balcony cluttered with old hanging laundry, today the apiary at the edge of the orchard . . . The first time, in the cabaret, wasn't there a woman singing? Was I the only one to hear a mute voice? And the Citadel tower fortified in the middle of the Plateaus, did I invent that as well? The beekeeper was not at the beehives.

I know the bees, I tamed them, as a child they loved only me, my mother was so surprised at my skill with the beekeeper of the interior gardens, which she had designed according to her whims so that only red flowers bloomed: poppies, camellias, geraniums, Sweet Williams, orchids, pomegranate flowers, amaryllis. In these gardens she read ancient poems to my father while he sat on the fountain stone.

My father often abandoned his young wife in the house with her servants, her gardens, her flowers, and her books. My father's library was famous in the region and beyond. Scholars came all the way from Asia Minor to consult the rare books. My mother, the only daughter, inherited the books that she read to my father, sometimes a servant listened to her, my father wouldn't shoo her away. My father used to say to my mother, "Your voice is beautiful, it attracts animals and young girls, no matter what you read." My mother loved the voice of the words mixed with the sound of the water. I also listened to her, hidden behind the pomegranate tree branches. Inside the trunk are the books that my mother read to my father. Protected. I think about these sacred books, these books of scholars, leather and gold, calligraphy, illuminations of color, astronomy, mathematics, law, grammar . . . Ancient manuscripts are eroded by the sands; libraries in the desert are not an infallible asylum. Abandoned in the grand house with no master, my mother's books will suffer the fate of books in the desert.

Between two rows of beehives, at the foot of a cypress tree, a young girl is singing. The Angel that doesn't accompany me didn't mislead me. The cabaret voice feels like the eucalyptus where the bees make their honey when the flowers are in bloom.

At the foot of the only ancient cypress, the beekeeper's daughter sings.

To die at this moment.

We looked everywhere for the body. Hundreds of men, in uniform, in civilian clothes, with bulletproof vests and hats, dispersed through the neighborhoods and hills of town. Weapons in hand, they searched the houses, palaces, villas, slums, apartments, towers, and complexes. An old woman approached the squad chief, a badge in her hand, swearing that she had discovered the body herself near the town, in a ravine, under the oleanders. The chief took the badge, he slid it into his pocket, he shooed the old woman away calling her crazy, he threatened to lock her up if she didn't disappear. The old woman left, shaking her cane at the squad chief.

That same evening, the national funerals of the Supreme Leader were announced on television. The ceremony would be a live broadcast.

The cortège didn't make it to the cemetery wall, for already the coffin was lifted by the crowd, passed from hand to hand, as if sucked up by the screaming bodies, then pushed along the crest. He reappeared, then disappeared farther away, floating in reverse, up to the small courtyard of a house made of corrugated metal where the gathered women, vigilant, formed a barrier that the praetorian guard wouldn't break through.

The coffin is a sarcophagus. The women look at it, dazzled.

Not a single one speaks. The precious wood, fragrant cedar, sacred, eternal, is sculpted, inlaid with pearls, decorated with gold leaf. The women don't know the meaning of the poem's golden letters inscribed on the wall of the sarcophagus, profane verses or divine words, it doesn't matter. The women don't remain quiet for long.

There is no longer the slightest sliver of gold on the cedar wood. The walls are smooth. One of the women goes into a lower chamber and returns with a hatchet. The dull murmurs. With the first blow, the women begin to shout in encouragement at the sacrilegious action. The woman strikes again and again. The coffin is empty.

103

I no longer live in the room in the red-light district. Sometimes I pass by, I water the Sweet Williams, I take a book, I lie down for a moment on the hard, narrow bed, I don't stay there.

They haven't given up on killing me.

It's that time when the streets are empty. It's nighttime. When I open the door to the room, I smell a feminine scent. I had forgotten that a woman smells like a woman, it's at the same time soft, sour, and bitter. That scent excites and nauseates me. I make a fist to quell a kind of rage that I leave unexplained.

The electricity has been cut off. The wooden blinds were left open. I glimpse a red ridge at the edge of the window. A woman is lying on my bed. She is sleeping.

104

I didn't think that a woman . . .

105

What if this woman was the singer?

To abandon the room, the cedar trunk, the red Sweet Williams.

They won't have any books.

106

The window is open. A woman is singing in my room. I listen to her until the evening.

An official car waits on her, the chauffeur is getting impatient, boys are throwing rocks at the doors, first from afar but then getting nearer and nearer, they see the woman, the car starts up and drives through the group of children in the middle of the road.

The coffin was not destroyed. The bronze locks remain intact. The falcons carved into the cedar aren't ruined. I know that the coffin shouldn't have left the ancestral house, I've always known that. My grandmother had put my mother on watch, she was not to lose the key, if someone were to open the coffin, the house and the family would be in danger. The coffin had been made by a town artisan, the best one.

The ancestor had supplied the wood from the ancient tree, the tree handed down from father to son. He had sacrificed the cedar to make the coffin as a gift to his favorite daughter when she married, the sacred coffin of the young virgin for whom a black rooster had been sacrificed, the most handsome and the most virile rooster on the farm. People say that a freed black slave had collected the blood of the beast and then coated the interior of the coffin with it, the young wife would therefore be protected by the red animals and the vermilion letters painted on the walls. The ancestor himself had drawn the falcons, he intended his daughter for the best hunter in the region, his father raised horses and falcons, at a very young age he began hunting, horseback riding, and fighting.

But nothing happened according to plan, and the coffin that should have remained for eternity in my mother's room is now in the room of a murderer in the red-light district.

107

The window remains open day and night. I watch her through the red carnations. She is sleeping. Did she drink a potion?

I love her scent.

108

My father is stretched out under the tree. Dead.

At first I don't realize it's my father, I don't realize that this man dressed in a soldier's uniform, his head and feet bare, had just been killed. The ones who are guarding the body talk among themselves, they keep saying, "An example must be made. The men aren't here, it's just old men, women, and children. The women will speak to their fathers, husbands, and brothers."

The women will talk, between shouts and tears, about the body in the little square, abandoned by the guards who don't respect God. They'll talk about the body exposed day and night until the village reeks, and then thrown with the other rotting carcasses into the ravine. Who will go fight the hyenas for the body among the bitter laurels and the thorns?

The guards watching the murdered man's corpse continue to say, "That man there, people say he was a lion. The boldest, the most cunning. He knew every rock, every bush in the Plateaus, all the hiding places and caves. The traps, that was him; stolen horses, that was him; the murderous ambushes, the victorious attack of armored vehicles, that was him; always ahead, a crazy warrior, a gang leader more efficient than a toughened head of state. He didn't die in combat . . ."

My mother's shrieks informed me that the man was my father. The soldiers stand guard around the body, one of them holds my mother still against the low wall, threatening with his weapon, my mother no longer moves but continues to scream, standing, she presses my head to her thigh, I'm trembling, she is too, I can feel her shaking from her mouth all the way to the soles of her feet. Did my mother know what was being said? And did she know why this man, dead under the tree, her beloved husband, had been shot down by his own men?

109

The room is empty.

They'll be there for me. The singer, if it's her, is an accomplice.

110

In this way, God wants chaos, torture, terror. Despair. God wants the Apocalypse. We will be the first to accomplish the divine will.

111

I saw a woman at my window. I'm the one she's waiting for.

A woman is still waiting for the Day of Judgment.

During the reign of Sheba, Solomon sent a letter, pinned to a hoopoe's beak.

Who is unaware of the crimes committed by the Police of the Police?

Who is unaware that certain groups are killing in the name of God?

God

The Merciful

The Knowing

The Seeing

The Fair

The Generous

The Wise

The Only One

The Pure

The Light

The Honest

The Patient

In this form I could recite all ninety-nine names of God, my mother taught them to me. It's said that the hundredth name is ineffable, God keeps it secret. I've imagined it, I've never written it down.

I'm being hunted. They're hunting for me. The Police are hunting for me. But I am far away.

113

My mother didn't know her father's grandfather, the one who bought the Sudanese slave at the big town market. The girl and the girl's child died in the master's house having never stepped outside. My mother kept the last girl from that family very close to her, today nobody knows who the fathers of these girls are.

I've always known the freed slave's girl, she was younger than my mother, whom she served, I don't know if she's still close to her after these years of disorder and silence.

I don't know if she followed her on her mad journeys across the steppe, the rocks, the High Plains and the ravines, sleeping in the caves, scratching the ground like a beast, drinking rainwater, speaking with gazelles and hyenas. A cheetah could have run toward her at twilight, and she wouldn't have been afraid. The young black woman watched over my mother, she whispered, "Mistress, you have a son, don't forget, your son is waiting in the house, your son is not yet a man . . . Return with me, mistress, I beg of you." My mother listened to the soft whisper, she didn't hear the words. I left before she returned. I didn't know that it was possible she might not return. Did the young servant bury her alone under the oleander? According to the ritual?

She loved my mother and my mother loved her. With my father gone, the young black woman never again left my mother's side.

My mother's hair. In order to see it without her scarves, I had to surprise her in her room very early in the morning, which I was forbidden to do, or in the public bath, where I only saw it wet, knotted in a bun at the nape of her neck, or at night while she prepared to lie down on the leather bed, tall and wide, reserved for my father and for her. If my father wasn't there, I didn't enter my mother's room, nor did her black servant, my mother's favorite.

My mother sat down on the sofa in the room next to her bedroom and the young girl styled her hair. Then I saw my mother veiled in smooth black, shining, moving, covered to her ankles. When the master of ceremony permitted it, I approached my mother who was hidden under her own hair, and before hugging her, I touched the animal fleece, doubting that a woman, my mother, would present her cheek to me. The servant laughed at my shyness; my mother, patient, waited for the morning kiss, the ebony comb threatened me if I lingered too long under the veil.

The servant styled my mother's hair with devotion. She spoke to my mother just as much as to her hair, she made up verses that glorified her beauty, her strength, her perfume. For the ritual, she burned incense in a small old urn that she had mysteriously found, she never wanted to reveal its origin.

My mother was getting impatient.

The young black woman braided and unbraided her hair for the pleasure of passing the comb from her head to her ankle. She compared my mother's hair to her own, short and frizzy, she said that she didn't like her own hair. My mother laughed while passing her hand over the thick mane, she said, "But it's soft, it's like the wool of a little black sheep, it's nice, and you don't suffer from migraines like I do . . . My hair weighs more than my body, sometimes I can't stand it . . . Here, this time it's decided, I'll cut my hair . . . Give me scissors or a sharp knife, do you hear me? I know, I know, the master will be angry, he's the one that forbids me from cutting my hair, I know, he loves it, he says it's my mane, his fur; he says it's the sea, the waves, its scent; he says it's like he's galloping along the Plateaus, my hair shaped like a star on the bed, on the fine wool carpet . . . But as for me, while he's gone, I can't stand this hair anymore . . . If you don't give me the scissors I'll get them myself, like women during the days of mourning in the absence of the master, for me it's like that . . ."

The servant interrupts her mistress, she plugs her ears, she cries, "Enough, enough! You don't have the right, this hair doesn't belong to you, the master is the one who decides . . . If you cut it he will kill you . . . He said it one day, I heard him."

My mother responds, "So you listen at the door to my room? Aren't you ashamed? If I cut my hair I'll give it to you."

The young girl, panic-stricken, screams again. "No, no, never, you never take dead hair, it's bad luck, you know that, mistress. I love your hair alive with you alive."

She resumed her ritualistic actions. I'm sitting at my mother's feet on the fine woolen rug, near the urn holding burning incense from Arabia. She braids the long hair, infatuated, she mixes in strands of red wool to the locks of hair. While she braids she leans toward my mother to touch the thick knot where the strands cross, she speaks into her ear, my mother laughs the way I sometimes hear her laugh with my father, she looks at the braid, she strokes the silky hollows, they look at each other, they laugh. I ask why they laugh. "You'll know when you're older . . . And anyway you shouldn't be here, you're too old to help with your mother's bathing . . . Mistress, what are you telling your son?"

I protest, "She says I'm too young and then that I'm too old."

My mother strokes my hair, it's short and curly, she says, "He has beautiful hair like his father." She stands up, and her braids disappear under the scarves.

114

The beauty is sleeping, I see her through the curly red carnations.

If she is an accomplice, I should be dead or in prison. If she isn't complicit, she's still an accomplice. Is she also waiting for me to wake her up?

Maybe she's the singer from the cabaret, I don't know. Before going to sleep she burned some incense, but against what curse? We are all damned.

I won't ever come back.

115

The news was not made public.

The body was found at the foot of a ravine, between

oleanders and thorns, ripped apart by vultures, partly devoured by hyenas. It was identified thanks to a secret amulet that the predators hadn't swallowed. The amulet that the victor of the revolt was wearing when they killed my father.

116

I went everywhere, into the cabarets, the secret rooms in the Palaces, the pleasure houses, the rooms in the forbidden villas reserved for torture when you refuse to fuck, these are called the love rooms.

The women are young and beautiful, refined. They're said to be well-read, poets and musicians. They sing and they dance, they smoke hashish like men, they get drunk on wine, perfumes, and song like men. They are accomplished courtesans.

Town councilors, unscrupulous businessmen, high-ranking officers, they all ruin themselves for the love of these women who know that they are murderers.

I'm looking for her where she isn't.

She's waiting for me in the room of the red-light district where I will no longer go.

At night, when I couldn't sleep, I got up and walked aimlessly, barefoot, from one courtyard to another through the underground tunnels and interior gardens, I avoided my mother's room but the birds in the cages informed her, their vigilance woke her, she looked for me, called for me softly, I went toward her, she took me in her arms and brought me to my room. "Why aren't you sleeping, my little one? A dream, a bad one? You should have called me. You know that I hear you even if you call me while I'm asleep, so tell me."

She sat on the bed where she laid me down under a light blanket, she said that she wove it for me before I was born with the wool from my father's sheep.

I asked for the story of Abraham and Ishmael. My mother repeated, "Again? But I've told it to you so many times. Why always this story? You don't want the one about Solomon and the queen of Sheba? Solomon was the one who spoke to the birds and the worms, the queen of Sheba was the daughter of an Asiatic prince and a magician. Solomon loved horses and women, like your father . . . He drank the sweat of his horses while he was hunting in the desert, he was the only one who knew that horse sweat is sweet and quenches your thirst . . ." I insisted, and my mother eventually gave in, "What more do you want to know? I've already told it to you, everything, you know the story by heart. Well . . . Abraham had received the order from God to kill his son Ishmael. Abraham put the child before him, drew the knife from his sleeve and, having pulled his son's head up to his breast, he began to cry."

I asked every time: "And Ishmael?" My mother responded, "Ishmael isn't afraid. He insists that his father accomplish the sacrifice, he advises his father to hide his face to facilitate the murderous action, Ishmael tells him that he must obey God. Abraham thus got up . . . He firmly tied up his son's hands, made him lie down on his right side and told him good-bye from the bottom of his heart. He loved his son, yes, he loved him. He wanted to put the knife to Ishmael's throat, but his hand was trembling and tears were streaming down his face . . . It's also said that when Abraham placed the knife on Ishmael's neck, the knife turned around; the sharp edge was found at the top and the handle at the bottom . . ."

My mother stopped reading, I asked her the same question. "And Ishmael?" "Ishmael asked his father to try again. Abraham did what his son said but at that moment God made Gabriel descend from the sky with a white ram . . . He had black eyes and long horns . . . Abraham said to Ishmael, 'Oh my son, raise your head, the hour of your deliverance has arrived.' When Ishmael raised his head, he saw Gabriel holding the ram and said, 'God is very great! Praise be to God!'"

My mother said, "You see, Abraham didn't kill Ishmael, he obeyed God who sent him the white ram. He didn't kill his son."

And I repeated, "Abraham put his knife on his son's throat, he was going to kill him, he wanted to kill his son, he didn't protect him, he didn't say no."

"If he had said no, Ishmael would have died anyway, and Abraham would be dead, and Ishmael wouldn't have had descendants . . . Do you understand?" I didn't respond. My mother read the story and I fell asleep.

118

I ran.

On the Plateaus I practiced the race with the son of my father's shepherd, I always won.

I know this town as if I had been born in it.

119

I'll return one last time to the room to leave this journal at the foot of the cedar trunk. I won't lock it.

"A trunk that's left open . . ." my grandmother used to say. The prophecy will be fulfilled.

I will be far away, beyond the grave.

120

My mother, what did she know?

She couldn't hear the men that talked in the square. They played dominos, young and old, they drank coffee, they gossiped, they did nothing else. Sitting to one side, I listened to them. First they spoke in low voices, then they forgot about the silent child at the other end of the small patio that barely protected them from the sun.

They didn't say his name but I knew that the hero was my father. He enforced military disciple with his men, excused no sign of weakness, always inflicting the cruelest retaliation. An extremist, said some, a hothead, a hero, a mystic . . . A madman who feared neither God nor death. Even those who admired him thought he had become dangerous.

The men who were playing dominoes stopped for a minute to try to agree on the most accurate story. Was he insane or not? Who could doubt his courage? Had he lacked judgment? Had a great, innocent man been killed? Some agreed with his actions, others accused him of extravagance. Some swore that his men loved him excessively, others that he was detested but feared. How can the truth be known, the players asked. The only surety that nobody contested is that one day he decided alone, without consulting the Counsel, to punish a soldier accused of treason. The soldier had deserted, they hadn't been able to find him. Like my father, he had lived in the Plateaus.

Three, five, seven days later, he had to gallop very far to find him, my father returned with the body of the deserter. My father found him hidden in a cave, he had noticed an acacia branch torn from arm's height at the edge of the path. They had fought at knifepoint. Again the players interrupted the game to argue about the details of that fight. My father fills the cave with smoke, the soldier comes out coughing, he recognizes the leader of the revolt, he's not afraid. Some say that he was too weak to defend himself, others say that my father gave him time to catch his breath. The fight was fair . . . The fight was uneven . . . The deserter was armed, my father too. They chose to duel at knifepoint. My father won.

With the traitor's body across his horse, my father arrived at the camp a triumphant victor. He didn't let anyone approach the dead man. Not even those on the Council with whom he hadn't consulted. He didn't speak, he didn't respond to orders, the Council threatened him, he said nothing. People say that his men who had waited for him didn't dare approach the horse, and that he would have killed anyone who was against him, he was like a madman. The men, standing by the tents, waited, resigned. The deserter was on the ground. My father searched everywhere in the camp, people let him, looking for a rope or wire. Using rope he attached the cadaver's ankles to his horse's tail. The body was naked.

The players didn't agree. How could the Council let him do such a thing? Why would he strip a dead soldier if he wasn't going to dress him in funeral clothes or a sheet? In war soldiers are buried the way they die, in uniform. This man was crazy to violate a corpse.

Was the traitor naked? My father jumped on his horse, he turned toward the dead deserter, he spoke to him, "This is how traitors should be punished. You died at my hand. Died once, and you'll die again, because you'll no longer have a face, and again, because you'll no longer be a man. At the end of the race, whoever looks at you won't recognize a human being, nor even an animal. You will be a monster because you committed a monstrous act. Nobody will prevent me from punishing you."

The horse left at a quick gallop, whipped by the wooden switch made from an olive tree, its flanks tight against the tan leather boots. The deserter's corpse, dragged along the stony ground, made countless rounds of the courtyard in the interior circle of military tents. The stunned rebels witnessed the torture of the dead, punctured by my father's vengeful shouts. When he stopped, my father drank the sweet sweat of his horse with his hands, he detached the bleeding body that was no longer a human body, he took it in his arms, he walked between two lines formed by his men, all the way to the ravine on the other side of the improvised campsite. Vultures went with him, flying high and screeching. My father walked alone between the thorns on the hills to the bottom of the ravine, the rebels stayed up on the edge, they watched the birds soaring over their prey. And he threw what was left of the deserter to the oleanders among the rocks. The vultures screeched.

My father returned alone to his tent, his men followed at a distance. People waited for him with a rope, he didn't struggle, they attached him to the trunk of a tree. He was shot. The revolt was subdued with the blood of the very one who would become the Supreme Leader.

The body of my father was exposed in the village square, his village, under the oak tree, barefoot.

My mother knew nothing. She wanted my father's body, that's all. She didn't ask questions. She loved him.

My father always returned.

This time my mother waited for him, she had a vague idea that he was in danger, my mother learned it by chance from the gossipers, the peddlers that still came by, the vagabonds, magicians, and clairvoyants spoke of the exploits and atrocities of a civil war, savage, invisible because my mother knew nothing.

My mother didn't hide, she no longer forbade me from her room, she barely knew that I was with her in the house, I saw her carry out strange actions with the complicity of her young servant. She spoke and at the same time chewed on pieces of paper, saying, "Please let him return one time, just once, don't let him be killed, only injured, I will treat him so he can return to combat. Don't let him abandon me in this house where I will die without him. Let him return alive, even if it's one last time. Let him hold me in his arms, so strong that I think I will melt into his heart, my heart pressing against his heart, my mouth against his mouth. My falcon . . . And let him enter me, whole."

My mother didn't laugh anymore, she kissed me without seeing me, she didn't cry, but I saw her wander around the house when she wasn't lying down for entire days in her leather bed, "her love bed," the young black girl called it; "my death bed," my mother called it. She hid messages under the cushions written in illegible words with characters I didn't know. They were magical formulas, without a doubt, my questions weren't answered, the black girl served my mother and her whims. The young girl left the house and returned to the room with ordinary objects that my mother made into precious objects: a plate with thick and indecipherable letters, which my mother polished morning and night, eggshells covered in inscriptions, was my mother going to eat them and suffocate? The bread made in the house also contained secret messages, my mother ate it in little pieces throughout the day, she fed herself with nothing but bread and honey. Her servant recited the directions with her, she prepared the embers to burn the pieces of paper, the letters, I was surprised there were so many, my mother must have been breathing in the smoke of the incense and the visionary vegetal fibers, she applied herself to reciting verses that spoke of love and death.

My father never returned. No news reached my mother's house. She persevered with her fumigations, she consumed the secret messages that she had delivered to her at night, she said that if she ever stopped my father would surely die.

Hearing the rumor, the servant, after returning from one of her nighttime expeditions, ran into my mother's room. At sunrise, a group of horsemen was seen heading toward the village. The master was at the head on a black stallion. My mother fainted. She didn't ask questions. She jumped from the bed where she had been resting day and night and began giving orders to the servants. The master should be honored like a master.

The bath was prepared; the sofa was decorated with the most vibrant silks; sweets were laid out on little tables, fruits, honey and almond cakes, sorbets, lemon, pomegranate, strawberry, sweet orange; incense and myrrh were burnt; the house smelled like roasted coffee. My mother had never been so beautiful. She kissed me, held me in her arms, "Your father is coming. God is merciful. Your father is alive. He has returned. God is great." My mother sat on the sofa and waited. The day passed, and then the night. Another day and a night. She touched neither the sweets nor the coffee despite the supplications of her tearful servant.

On the morning of the third day, she stumbled to her feet, took a small pointed knife and slashed the silks, the sofa, the rug, her ceremonial clothes. She turned over the garnished tables and stamped on the fruit and cakes. She screamed and called for the young black servant. When she was in front of her, my mother took a wooden switch made from an olive tree that my father had left on a trunk and she began to hit her, I tried to protect her but my mother struck without seeing, mad with anger. In each other's arms, we didn't move under the blows, my mother thrashed for as long as her rage gave her strength, then she slumped down, as if she had fainted. We laid her out on the ripped sofa; the servants—where were they until now?—came with basins of hot water and white honeycomb-woven towels. They didn't stop talking while they treated her, they talked about my mother like a crazy woman that would need to be watched over. Did they know that my father was on the road to his ruin? And that he would be shot by his own men a few days later?

My father loved his young wife, women, horses, war.

He died in infamy.

122

I am far away.

I live beyond the grave.

Others will come.

LEÏLA SEBBAR was born in 1941 to an Algerian father and a French mother. Much of her literature involves the relationship between France and Algeria, including direct juxtaposition of imagery related to both countries in order to highlight the differing cultures. A unique quality of her work is her penchant for keeping her characters unnamed. Her other translated works include *Sherazade*; *The Seine Was Red: Paris, October 1961*; and *Arabic as a Secret Song*.

RACHEL CROVELLO received early exposure to foreign languages at an immersion school and has been translating ever since. After specializing in Arabic and Translation Studies while completing her B.A. in Linguistics at Stanford University, she continues to dedicate herself to literary translation. This is her first book-length translation.

MICHAL AJVAZ, *The Golden Age.*
The Other City.

PIERRE ALBERT-BIROT, *Grabinoulor.*

YUZ ALESHKOVSKY, *Kangaroo.*

FELIPE ALFAU, *Chromos.*
Locos.

ANTÓNIO LOBO ANTUNES, *Knowledge of Hell.*
The Splendor of Portugal.

JOHN ASHBERY & JAMES SCHUYLER, *A Nest of Ninnies.*

ROBERT ASHLEY, *Perfect Lives.*

DJUNA BARNES, *Ladies Almanack.*
Ryder.

SVETISLAV BASARA, *Chinese Letter.*

MIQUEL BAUÇÀ, *The Siege in the Room.*

RENÉ BELLETTO, *Dying.*

MAREK BIENCZYK, *Transparency.*

ANDREI BITOV, *Pushkin House.*

ANDREJ BLATNIK, *You Do Understand.*
Law of Desire.

IGNÁCIO DE LOYOLA BRANDÃO, *Anonymous Celebrity.*
Zero.

BONNIE BREMSER, *Troia: Mexican Memoirs.*

GABRIELLE BURTON, *Heartbreak Hotel.*

MICHEL BUTOR, *Degrees.*
Mobile.

G. CABRERA INFANTE, *Infante's Inferno.*
Three Trapped Tigers.

JULIETA CAMPOS, *The Fear of Losing Eurydice.*

ANNE CARSON, *Eros the Bittersweet.*

MARIE CHAIX, *The Laurels of Lake Constance.*

HUGO CHARTERIS, *The Tide Is Right.*

ERIC CHEVILLARD, *Demolishing Nisard.*
The Author and Me.

MARC CHOLODENKO, *Mordechai Schamz.*

JOSHUA COHEN, *Witz.*

EMILY HOLMES COLEMAN, *The Shutter of Snow.*

ERIC CHEVILLARD, *The Author and Me.*

ROBERT COOVER, *A Night at the Movies.*

STANLEY CRAWFORD, *Log of the S.S. The Mrs Unguentine.*
Some Instructions to My Wife.

RENÉ CREVEL, *Putting My Foot in It.*

RALPH CUSACK, *Cadenza.*

NICHOLAS DELBANCO, *Sherbrookes.*
The Count of Concord.

NIGEL DENNIS, *Cards of Identity.*

PETER DIMOCK, *A Short Rhetoric for Leaving the Family.*

ARIEL DORFMAN, *Konfidenz.*

ARKADII DRAGOMOSHCHENKO, *Dust.*

JEAN ECHENOZ, *Chopin's Move.*

FRANÇOIS EMMANUEL, *Invitation to a Voyage.*

PAUL EMOND, *The Dance of a Sham.*

SALVADOR ESPRIU, *Ariadne in the Grotesque Labyrinth.*

JUAN FILLOY, *Op Oloop.*

ANDY FITCH, *Pop Poetics.*

GUSTAVE FLAUBERT, *Bouvard and Pécuchet.*

JON FOSSE, *Aliss at the Fire.*
Melancholy.

MAX FRISCH, *I'm Not Stiller.*
Man in the Holocene.

CARLOS FUENTES, *Christopher Unborn.*
Distant Relations.
Terra Nostra.
Where the Air Is Clear.

TAKEHIKO FUKUNAGA, *Flowers of Grass.*

WILLIAM GADDIS, JR., *The Recognitions.*

JANICE GALLOWAY, *Foreign Parts.*
The Trick Is to Keep Breathing.

WILLIAM H. GASS, *Life Sentences.*
The Tunnel.
The World Within the Word.
Willie Masters' Lonesome Wife.

GÉRARD GAVARRY, *Hoppla! 1 2 3..*

JIŘÍ GRUŠA, *The Questionnaire.*

AMANDA MICHALOPOULOU, *I'd Like.*

CHRISTINE MONTALBETTI, *The Origin of Man.*

DOROTHY NELSON, *In Night's City. Tar and Feathers.*

ESHKOL NEVO, *Homesick.*

WILFRIDO D. NOLLEDO, *But for the Lovers.*

BORIS A. NOVAK, *The Master of Insomnia.*

FLANN O'BRIEN, *At Swim-Two-Birds. The Best of Myles. The Dalkey Archive. The Hard Life. The Poor Mouth. The Third Policeman.*

CLAUDE OLLIER, *The Mise-en-Scène. Wert and the Life Without End.*

PATRIK OUŘEDNÍK, *Europeana. The Opportune Moment, 1855.*

BORIS PAHOR, *Necropolis.*

FERNANDO DEL PASO, *News from the Empire. Palinuro of Mexico.*

ROBERT PINGET, *The Inquisitory. Mahu or The Material. Trio.*

MANUEL PUIG, *Betrayed by Rita Hayworth. The Buenos Aires Affair. Heartbreak Tango.*

RAYMOND QUENEAU, *The Last Days. Odile. Pierrot Mon Ami. Saint Glinglin.*

ANN QUIN, *Berg. Passages. Three. Tripticks.*

ISHMAEL REED, *The Free-Lance Pallbearers. The Last Days of Louisiana Red. Ishmael Reed: The Plays. Juice! The Terrible Threes. The Terrible Twos.*

Yellow Back Radio Broke-Down.

JASIA REICHARDT, *15 Journeys Warsaw to London.*

JOÃO UBALDO RIBEIRO, *House of the Fortunate Buddhas.*

JEAN RICARDOU, *Place Names.*

RAINER MARIA RILKE, *The Notebooks of Malte Laurids Brigge.*

JULIÁN RÍOS, *The House of Ulysses. Larva: A Midsummer Night's Babel. Poundemonium.*

ALAIN ROBBE-GRILLET, *Project for a Revolution in New York. A Sentimental Novel.*

AUGUSTO ROA BASTOS, *I the Supreme.*

DANIËL ROBBERECHTS, *Arriving in Avignon.*

JEAN ROLIN, *The Explosion of the Radiator Hose.*

OLIVIER ROLIN, *Hotel Crystal.*

ALIX CLEO ROUBAUD, *Alix's Journal.*

JACQUES ROUBAUD, *The Form of a City Changes Faster, Alas, Than the Human Heart. The Great Fire of London. Hortense in Exile. Hortense Is Abducted. Mathematics: The Plurality of Worlds of Lewis. Some Thing Black.*

RAYMOND ROUSSEL, *Impressions of Africa.*

VEDRANA RUDAN, *Night.*

GERMAN SADULAEV, *The Maya Pill.*

TOMAŽ ŠALAMUN, *Soy Realidad.*

LYDIE SALVAYRE, *The Company of Ghosts. The Lecture. The Power of Flies.*

LUIS RAFAEL SÁNCHEZ, *Macho Camacho's Beat.*

SEVERO SARDUY, *Cobra & Maitreya.*

NATHALIE SARRAUTE, *Do You Hear Them? Martereau. The Planetarium.*

GERALD MURNANE, *Barley Patch.*
Inland.

YVES NAVARRE, *Our Share of Time.*
Sweet Tooth.

STIG SÆTERBAKKEN, *Siamese.*
Self-Control.
Through the Night.

ARNO SCHMIDT, *Collected Novellas.*
Collected Stories.
Nobodaddy's Children.
Two Novels.

ASAF SCHURR, *Motti.*

GAIL SCOTT, *My Paris.*

DAMION SEARLS, *What We Were Doing
and Where We Were Going.*

JUNE AKERS SEESE,
Is This What Other Women Feel Too?

BERNARD SHARE, *Inish.*
Transit.

VIKTOR SHKLOVSKY, *Bowstring.*
Literature and Cinematography.
Theory of Prose.
Third Factory.
Zoo, or Letters Not about Love.

PIERRE SINIAC, *The Collaborators.*

KJERSTI A. SKOMSVOLD,
The Faster I Walk, the Smaller I Am.

JOSEF ŠKVORECKÝ, *The Engineer of
Human Souls.*

GILBERT SORRENTINO, *Aberration of
Starlight.*
Blue Pastoral.
Crystal Vision.
Imaginative Qualities of Actual Things.
Mulligan Stew. Red the Fiend.
Steelwork.
Under the Shadow.

MARKO SOSIČ, *Ballerina, Ballerina.*

ANDRZEJ STASIUK, *Dukla.*
Fado.

GERTRUDE STEIN, *The Making of
Americans.*
A Novel of Thank You.

LARS SVENDSEN, *A Philosophy of Evil.*

PIOTR SZEWC, *Annihilation.*

GONÇALO M. TAVARES, *A Man: Klaus
Klump.*
Jerusalem.
Learning to Pray in the Age of Technique.

NIKANOR TERATOLOGEN, *Assisted
Living.*

TAEKO TOMIOKA, *Building Waves.*

JOHN TOOMEY, *Sleepwalker.*

DUMITRU TSEPENEAG, *Hotel Europa.*
The Necessary Marriage.
Pigeon Post.
Vain Art of the Fugue.

ESTHER TUSQUETS, *Stranded.*

DUBRAVKA UGRESIC, *Lend Me Your
Character.*
Thank You for Not Reading.

TOR ULVEN, *Replacement.*

MATI UNT, *Brecht at Night.*
Diary of a Blood Donor.
Things in the Night.

ÁLVARO URIBE & OLIVIA SEARS, EDS.,
Best of Contemporary Mexican Fiction.

ELOY URROZ, *Friction.*
The Obstacles.

LUISA VALENZUELA, *Dark Desires and
the Others.*
He Who Searches.

PAUL VERHAEGHEN, *Omega Minor.*

BORIS VIAN, *Heartsnatcher.*

MARGUERITE YOUNG, *Angel in the
Forest.*
Miss MacIntosh, My Darling.

REYOUNG, *Unbabbling.*

VLADO ŽABOT, *The Succubus.*

ZORAN ŽIVKOVIĆ , *Hidden Camera.*

LOUIS ZUKOFSKY, *Collected Fiction.*

VITOMIL ZUPAN, *Minuet for Guitar.*

SCOTT ZWIREN, *God Head.*

AND MORE . . .